The Mosquito Brothers

The Mosquito Brothers

GRIFFIN ONDAATJE

ILLUSTRATIONS BY
Erica Salcedo

GROUNDWOOD BOOKS
HOUSE OF ANANSI PRESS
TORONTO   BERKELEY

The Mosquito Brothers is a work of fiction. Any resemblance to individual mosquitoes, walking or flying, is purely coincidental.

Groundwood Books / House of Anansi Press
110 Spadina Avenue, Suite 801, Toronto, Ontario M5V 2K4
or c/o Publishers Group West
1700 Fourth Street, Berkeley CA 94710

We acknowledge for their financial support of our publishing program the Canada Council for the Arts, the Government of Canada through the Canada Book Fund (CBF) and the Ontario Arts Council.

**Canada Council
for the Arts** **Conseil des Arts
du Canada**

**ONTARIO ARTS COUNCIL
CONSEIL DES ARTS DE L'ONTARIO**
an Ontario government agency
un organisme du gouvernement de l'Ontario

Library and Archives Canada Cataloguing in Publication
Ondaatje, Griffin, author
The mosquito brothers / written by Griffin Ondaatje ; illustrations by Erica Salcedo.
Issued in print and electronic formats.
ISBN 978-1-55498-437-4 (bound).—ISBN 978-1-55498-439-8 (html).
—ISBN 978-1-55498-827-3 (mobi)
I. Salcedo, Erica, illustrator II. Title.
PS8629.N38M68 2015   jC813'.6   C2014-906787-9
C2014-906788-7

Cover illustration by Erica Salcedo
Design by Michael Solomon

Printed and bound in Canada

FSC
www.fsc.org
MIX
Paper from
responsible sources
FSC® C016245

For Lilla, Calin and Akash.

✷

For Sang-Mi.
For Si.
And for Christopher, my best friend growing up.

"What I say may be very small . . ."
— The Mighty Sparrow

Contents

PART I
Home City

The Parking Lot

He was born in a puddle at the back row of the parking lot of the Lakeside Drive-In Theater, along with his four hundred brothers and sisters.

His name was Dinn. Dinn Needles. His mother decided to spell his name with three Ns. She already had another child named Dinn (with two Ns), and she was tired of thinking up new names.

When he was four seconds old, Dinn flew away from the small egg raft he shared with his brothers and sisters and fell sideways into the water. He almost drowned. His mother saw the little splash he made and flew down. She brushed him with her wings so he floated up to the cloud of other hatched mosquitoes hovering above the wide and dirty puddle.

For two long seconds Dinn tried to stay amid his hundreds of siblings. But he was unusually skinny, even for a mosquito. In all the commotion, he was

jostled and bumped and couldn't see where he was going. Scared of falling underwater again, he elbowed his way through the swarm and tumbled onto the ground, rolling into the dust just beyond the edge of the puddle.

From that second onward, Dinnn gave up trying to fly. He was not good at flying, he told himself. So he decided to walk wherever he had to go.

❈

Dinnn spent the first few sunny days of spring walking around the empty parking lot. He learned on his own how to lean and sip sweet water from trampled candy wrappers, bottle caps and flowers in the flat grass near the garbage cans.

One morning he woke up before dawn. That way he could get a head start to wherever his siblings were flying that day. For the first hour or so, Dinnn walked in darkness. By the time he reached the road, the sun was up. Moving slowly on his six legs, he felt the warm sun on his back.

Suddenly, he heard his brothers and sisters coming up behind him. They buzzed overhead. A few hundred of them quickly passed.

A couple of the slower ones called down, "Hey, weirdo. Crawl back home."

They never slowed down to be with him, and they pretended not to know him when other bugs were around. His siblings were embarrassed to have a brother who walked everywhere.

But Dinnn didn't mind having to walk in the dust or make his way around puddles.

What's the big deal? he thought. I just take a little longer.

❃

One morning, as the orange sun rose behind the drive-in theater, Dinnn looked at the sky.

I wish the sky wasn't so high up, he thought.

His nose trembled as he watched the clouds move fast above him. The thought of leaving the ground terrified him. Leaving the ground would mean letting go — plummeting into the sky.

Insects crisscrossed the air from the garbage dump all the way to the lake. All of them seemed to know something Dinnn didn't.

He kept thinking about the day he was born. He stared beyond his nose at the clouds, remembering the exact moment he fell into that puddle.

Dinnn could never shake that awful feeling of falling, and of being left behind.

And so each morning he walked beside the road. He

walked to school, his light wings resting on his back.

Meanwhile, all the other young mosquitoes caught the gentle breeze. They floated up above the gravel and drifted over the grass.

At the insect crosswalk, the crossing guard — an old ladybug — made Dinnn stand and wait, even though the road was always empty. Dinnn hunched his shoulders, waiting for her whistle to chirp. Then he walked across the road.

Finally he walked down into the ditch, toward the

old discarded air conditioner that was the local school for mosquitoes.

He usually arrived late. Instead of flying through the front vent like the other mosquitoes, Dinnn walked around the side and crawled through a hole in the air filter. Then he sat in the very back row. He sat with his skinny hind legs stretched out, acting "cool."

But he wasn't cool at all, and the other mosquitoes could tell.

❋

One afternoon, walking home along the side of the road, Dinnn found a dusty old black leather jacket lying in the ditch.

He picked it up.

This looks cool, he thought.

On the back of the jacket were words:

THE

WASP

BROTHERS

Dinnn looked up and down the road to see if anyone was watching. Then he tried the jacket on. It was far too big, but it hung on his shoulders well enough, covering his wings. Still, it was so heavy that Dinnn walked even more slowly than before.

He wore the jacket the whole day. He never took it off, not even to sleep.

※

One day he asked his mother if she could change a word on his jacket. His mother didn't know how to sew, and she couldn't see that well, but she picked and poked at the threads with her long sharp nose.

When she was finished, the words said:

THE
MOSQUITO
BROTHERS

Perfect, Dinnn thought. He would be one of the cool mosquitoes now.

He wore the jacket all the time. He got used to its weight, and he always walked along slowly, even when his teachers — or his mother and father — told him he should try flying.

And after a while everyone got used to Dinnn not flying at all. Even his parents stopped asking him to fly.

※

But Dinnn was still lonely on the ground.

Some nights he watched flurries of moths and night beetles around streetlights. Even grasshoppers leapt through the glow. The silent blizzard of insects looked beautiful.

Once, out of nowhere, he saw a bat swoop down and scatter the moths like snowflakes.

His brothers and sisters hovered near the lights, too, sometimes until dawn. Dinnn watched and waited for them. All night he stood in the towering grass. His oldest brothers were usually the last to return. He saw them make a soft touchdown, their long legs absorbing the impact.

They didn't even notice him waiting there. They didn't notice his jacket.

It's Hard to Be a Mosquito
in the City

WITH HUNDREDS of kids to take care of, Dinnn's mother and father were busy and tired all the time. His father was a little less busy, but he was more tired than his mother. He was more tired because the late show at the drive-in started at nine o'clock every night. Dinnn's father would bolt up and fly across the parking lot to the big screen. It shone there like a square moon. He couldn't help himself. He loved to go close to the swirling dots of color and dancing lights.

Hours later, when he fluttered home, his eyes were red, and he was so tired he couldn't even look for work. Instead he slept on a leaf floating at the edge of their puddle all day.

❋

Whenever it rained along their road, Dinnn would

stand in the bus shelter. He would wait there, hoping the other mosquitoes would notice his leather jacket.

Once, a small mosquito sitting on the curb looked over and stared at his jacket, but Dinn pretended not to notice. He tried to pretend he was going somewhere. He looked into the distance, squinting. The big teenage mosquitoes floated up to roof corners and dared one another to fly close to the spider webs.

Dinn kept to himself. There was a lot to worry about as a flightless mosquito on the ground. Big teenagers and spider webs weren't the only things that made him tense.

One quiet afternoon, as the family sat next to their puddle under a cloudless sky, Dinn heard a dragonfly flying overhead. It made a loud, awful sound as it went past.

Dinn watched the faces of his mother and father closely. They were terrified.

Dragonflies rarely entered the city, but Dinn knew from stories his parents had told him that they flew incredibly fast. And, of course, they ate mosquitoes. Dinn was glad then that he couldn't fly. While the others played games, he kept an eye out for dragonflies at all times.

Dinn was always on the lookout. During a family picnic in the grass at the edge of the parking lot, he watched a dozen of his sisters fly up to a telephone wire where a pigeon was dozing. They flew higher than they ever had before. Higher than a house.

His whole family watched them dive in and out gracefully, taking turns biting the drowsy bird. They seemed so dangerously high, in sight of any dragonfly that might be roaming around.

Dinnn could barely stand to watch.

✳

One rainy evening, Dinnn's whole family rose off the puddle and took shelter in a big maple tree. Dinnn followed them, climbing up the trunk as fast as he could. The wind blew wildly, and when lightning flashed, Dinnn hid behind his four hundred brothers and sisters. He peered out from behind their backs to glimpse the angry branches of light. Thunder crashed.

To Dinnn, the bolts of lightning looked like the wings of giant dragonflies searching for him in the dark.

The storm went on all night. To pass the time, their father told them about the movies he saw at the drive-in. As his siblings drifted in and out of sleep in the tree, Dinnn listened to every word.

❋

The next morning the parking lot was covered in water. Dinnn climbed down the tree. He walked around a giant puddle and got lost in the tall grass by the road. He couldn't find his way out of the ditch.

A few teenage mosquitoes circled over him, laughing.

Finally, his mother floated over and guided him to dry ground.

"I'm okay, Mom. Just fly home," Dinnn whispered.

His mother patted his head and flew off.

The teenagers drifted back toward Dinnn.

"Mommy go bye-bye!" one taunted. Then they all flew down the road.

❋

Dinnn felt there must be something more for him. Something he was meant to do, some place he was meant to go.

But where? he thought.

When the weekend came, his brothers and sisters flew down the road past the city dump to the automated car wash. It was the only place open within a hundred yards.

Dinnn decided to follow, crawling along in his heavy, thick jacket.

It took him the whole morning to get to the car wash. When he finally arrived, his siblings had already left. He stood there alone and watched the cars go through one at a time. Water jets sprayed and wind dryers blew against the windshields.

Dinnn watched it all. He dreamed about going somewhere fast in a car one day.

The next time his brothers and sisters went to the car wash, Dinnn walked in the other direction. He went to the south end of the parking lot, toward the lake.

He was determined to see something new, to find adventure.

When he got to the edge of the parking lot, he saw a grain of sand blowing across the asphalt. It rolled toward him.

Suddenly it bounced up and crashed against his knee and knocked him over. A few sand flies lifted their heads. They pointed at him, laughing.

Dinnn got up and dusted off his jacket. This was not the way to find adventure.

"I should be flying. I'm almost two weeks old!" he muttered.

He turned and headed back toward the puddle.

Whenever Dinnn felt lost and alone, it made him feel better to hear his parents tell stories.

Maybe it was time to ask them again how he came to be born here in a parking lot . . .

The Story of Corrina Culiseta-Woo and Brad Needles

DINNN'S PARENTS weren't from the city.

His father couldn't remember much. He was an orphan, and his name was Brad Needles.

"There's not much to my story," he said. "I grew up in a gas station an hour out of the city." The gas station was on the highway, but Dinnn's father didn't know exactly where.

"It wasn't a big rest stop or anything," he said. His father always had a dreamy, faraway look in his eyes when he spoke of the gas station. "It had the most beautiful neon sign," he would say.

Dinnn's mother was born in the countryside — far away — inside an old tractor tire beside a swamp. She came from an especially big family. Her name was

Corrina Culiseta-Woo. The land where she grew up was a three-hour car drive from the parking lot.

"I remember those sweet country evenings," she said, sitting by the puddle. "How beautiful it all was."

His mother paused, lost in thought for a moment. She looked down at Dinnn gently.

"You know, Dinnn, I've haven't told you this, but you have a half brother back there in the Wild." Her face looked sad. "I used to sing him a song about rain when he was little," she said softly.

"Mom?" Dinnn said, a little worried.

"Yes?"

"What happened?"

His mother stared far into the distance.

"It was long, long ago. Over sixty days now." She touched the water gently with her foreleg, creating a ripple. "I was young, watching over my first batch of eggs. A raft of 111 little ones. They floated side by side in the rainwater in our tire swing."

She looked down sadly at the puddle.

"Their father was from a swamp a hundred yards away. His head was full of dreams. He was a bit like your dad. When our newborns started flying, he promised to hover over them."

She stared at the water, her eyes becoming hazy.

"I needed a blood meal, so I left the kids with him.

But he took off for Muskoka. When I came back minutes later, I discovered there had been a ferocious attack by two pondhawk dragonflies. Many families were wiped out. I searched the tire but our young ones were . . . gone.”

His mother suddenly began to cry, and she turned away from Dinnn.

“All except one,” she said.

Dinnn stared at his mother. He didn’t know what to think.

I have a brother in the Wild? he thought. And he survived a dragonfly attack?

After a while Corrina turned around again. She smiled at Dinnn.

“I hope one day all of us can be together.”

Dinnn nodded, but he didn’t speak. He just thought about the young mosquito — his brother who had survived a dragonfly attack. Hiding alone at the bottom of a dark, empty tire.

Dinnn’s mother straightened and wiped her antennae. She sat on the grass and took a breath and continued her story.

“One afternoon, days later, a car parked below the big pine tree where I lived with my little son in a knothole. We were with relatives. We had all drunk a lot of plant juice and sap, and we were dozing high in the tree. For some reason, I woke, and I knew something was in the air . . . "

She paused and scratched her nose with her forelegs.

"I *smelled* the car first, really," she said. "Gas fumes floated off its hood. It was a city car. A red minivan. I was curious, so I flew under the engine and crawled inside an air vent that led to the dashboard by the front passenger seat."

Corrina told Dinnn that she explored the inside of the car and lost track of time for several minutes, humming and bouncing against the windows.

Then the car started to move away from the tree.

"My family heard the engine," she said. "They all came and swarmed around the rear window. I flew against the glass. But they couldn't hear me crying out for my son . . . "

She met Dinnn's father an hour later when the car pulled up at a gas station along the highway.

It was dark, and there was a flashing neon sign: GAS FOR SALE.

Dinnn's future father was hovering above it, buzzing around with a few thousand of his friends. They were all high up in the clear evening sky, in a giant swarm, watching headlights pass on the highway. Most of the swarm were what Corrina's mother would have called floaters. ("Floaters," her mom said, "will hang around any bright light.")

Dinnn's father was a floater if ever there was one.

When the driver's window opened, Corrina flew into the night, higher and higher. She made a high-pitched whine as she headed toward the nearest trees. She was aiming for a constellation of stars that she recognized from home.

She felt something tug one of her legs. When she looked down, she saw a nervous-looking mosquito.

"Hey! Where are you going?" the jittery mosquito asked.

"What?"

"You flying to the moon or something?" He was shivering in the cold air, his big round eyes staring and his wings beating wildly. He had never been this high before, and it took all his energy.

"I'm trying to get home to my family."

Corrina could hear that he was out of breath. She slowed her wings so they buzzed at the same speed as his.

The two hovered in the big sky. He kept moving between her and the moon, shifting expectantly from side to side. It was then, while his shivering silhouette floated between her and the sky — his shoulders and wings pumping up and down in front of the yellow moon — that Corrina fell in love. She fell in love with the last mosquito her mother would have wanted for her. A floater by the highway!

Brad Needles had fallen in love, too. Mosquitoes, on average, fall in love very quickly, and he was an average mosquito. To him, Corrina was the most beautiful mosquito north of the highway.

Soon Corrina and Brad floated down through the sky together, gliding past the trees. In the blue glow of the GAS FOR SALE sign they got married and were swarmed by well-wishers.

It all happened so fast. Brad began to introduce Corrina to his friends one by one.

Suddenly, below them, Corrina heard the car engine start again.

"We have to go!" Corrina cried. "That minivan is the only way I'll find my way home again!"

She and Brad flew to the front window, and they made it in just as it shut.

"We continued west to the big city, away from home," she told Dinnn. Her eyes went soft as she looked at the sun setting. "West with the night."

By late evening the red minivan had reached the outskirts of town and passed through suburbs. It drove downtown where there were only a few skinny trees, and finally to the harbor where there was a house by the lake with one big maple tree. There was a parking lot, and at the far end of the parking lot a dazzling fifty-foot movie screen shone brightly.

Neither of them had ever seen such a sight.

When the car parked and a door opened, Corrina and Brad flew up into the maple.

"What's that big square light over there, Corrina?" Brad said. He was panting in the leaves, shifting back and forth, peering into the distance.

"I don't know," Corrina said. "But let's stay away from it for now."

"No way!"

Brad grabbed Corrina's foreleg and pulled her into the open air. They flew over the parked cars toward the gigantic screen.

And when they landed on it, it was like they had landed on the moon.

Brad looked at Corrina and smiled. She looked at him and smiled. They were glowing in light. And in love.

A week later their four hundred children were born. And everything changed.

Stillwater School
for Mosquitoes

ACTUALLY, 401 children were born: 200 girls and 201 boys. Dinnn — the final pupa to hatch — was always overlooked because he stayed on the ground.

School started the week Dinnn was born. His mother flew around like crazy making arrangements. Dinnn's father sat in the school office for two days filling out registration leaves, but so many of his kids had pesticide allergies that the paperwork took all his energy, and he fell asleep in the hall by the juice machine.

On the first day, the biology teacher droned on and on about the life cycles of mosquitoes.

"In our lifetimes we go on a complex journey from egg to larva to pupa to imago, or adult. It's truly a miraculous *circle of life!*" Their teacher always got very excited when he repeated the four-stage cycle, over and over, to each new class.

❋

After Dinnn heard his mother's story, he began to dream about going to the country one day — to the Wild, where his half brother lived. He wondered how long it would take him to walk there.

One day, he asked the only insect smart enough to know: Mr. Bluebottle, his math teacher.

Mr. Bluebottle was an old housefly. It was said he'd once flown on a plane, in a crate full of smoked salmon.

"You mosquitoes are slow flyers to begin with," the teacher said, buzzing across the room. "Slower than butterflies." He calculated that a three-hour car drive would be (wind permitting) a seven-day nonstop flight for a grown mosquito, at a top speed of two miles per hour.

"There's no way you could ever fly that far, Dinnn. Even if you weren't wearing that jacket. Walking that distance would take you 6.5 lifetimes."

Dinnn stared into his teacher's glinting multisided eyes.

"Oh. Well, thanks anyway, Mr. Bluebottle, I guess," he said.

❋

At Stillwater School, Dinnn always paid attention whenever a teacher mentioned dragonflies. Even though no one had seen dragonflies in the city for months, the students were instructed about the dangers.

Dragonflies had huge eyes, a long thorax, four wings, sharp jaws and weird digestive systems. Sometimes the school even held Dragonfly Drills in case of an emergency.

One day after school, a circle of teenage mosquitoes hovered over Dinnn as he climbed out of the ditch.

"Hey, speedy, what's your hurry? Dragonflies chasing ya?"

They all laughed.

"Don't worry," another said. "If dragonflies attack, you're a perfect target. You won't know what hit ya!"

One landed and imitated Dinnn walking slowly.

"You may as well change your jacket from Mosquito Brothers to Mosquito Breakfast! Ha ha ha!"

Dinnn pretended not to hear. He thought of his half brother alone in the Wild, fighting off dragonflies.

He wished he were here now. His brother would understand how it felt to be alone.

All the way home, Dinnn pretended his brother from the Wild was with him, walking beside him, telling him not to be afraid.

The 100-Million-Year Lecture

AT STILLWATER SCHOOL, young mosquitoes learned to cope with the challenges of insect life. "Mosquitoes: Surviving Our First 100 Million Years" was taught by a teacher who knew modern dangers better than any other bug. Mr. Proudnose had a radical theory. The real enemies of mosquitoes, he suggested, were *everyday objects*.

Proudnose despised human inventions, and his most despised invention was glass. He hated glass for a reason. His wife and 170 of his children had been squished while watching TV through the window of an electronics store.

Proudnose was known for long speeches. At the start of his lecture he stood for three long seconds with wings folded, staring through a vent.

A fluffy dandelion seed drifted in and began to float slowly down.

"Windows are the most devious invention of all time!" Mr. Proudnose suddenly shouted. His wings stirred the air, causing the dandelion seed to rise. "Glass, to be precise."

"Glass?" a student asked.

"Yes! Sweet, innocent, harmless *glass*," he said sarcastically. "It's like a wall of solid air. It doesn't move. Yet by the end of this week, one in five of you will be squashed looking through a glass window."

A few of the older students stifled laughter.

"Danger comes out of nowhere! Remember that! One of my cousins visited a farm and was killed on the side of the road. Inhaled by a cow!"

Dinnn raised his foreleg.

"Why is a mosquito's life so . . . short?"

"Short! What's time to a mosquito?" Proudnose responded abruptly. He pushed the floating dandelion seed out of his way. "So what if mosquitoes don't live what humans call a *long* life? There's sea grass in the Mediterranean that's 200,000 years old, for crying out loud!"

He calmed down and looked out the vent again.

"My ancestors followed tourists out of the Grand Canyon and hitchhiked through a desert. They saw highways sparkling like diamonds in the moonlight. In Utah my great-grandmother landed on a tree colony 80,000 years old — just before she was eaten by a purple martin. But for one timeless second she stood on top of the oldest living organism on earth!"

"But how can we survive in a world so much bigger than us?"

"Bigger?" Proudnose yelled. "What does big mean to a mosquito? My aunt in Sri Lanka once landed on a blue whale. It was one hundred feet long. She barely had time to bite, but she got the job done, her weight tripling with blood. And that whale went on to swim through the seven seas. Similarly, we mosquitoes are free to fly through any open window on the planet. We remain the most dangerous animal the world has ever known. For 100 million years we've dominated the earth. Today we have over 3,500 recognized species working around the clock 365 days a year in two hemispheres. Companies spend millions on insect repellents every day. But still we prevail. Humans may have silly inventions like glass. But we have the power to pester them to total distraction."

A few students giggled.

"You laugh, but in prehistoric times we forced humankind's ancestors back into caves until they huddled around campfires. When we showed up at dusk, cave people dropped whatever they were doing to fight us."

Proudnose paced with renewed energy.

"We've attended almost every important outdoor event in history. We've enjoyed fine dining at Buckingham Palace, the Taj Mahal and the White House! Our ancestors have slipped freely over castle walls, borders and front porches for hundreds of generations. In wartime we have turned back whole armies, forcing generals to redraw plans of global conquest. As I speak there are giant gallinipper mosquitoes the size of bottle caps invading Florida! We've survived missions to outer space — one of our kind clinging for a year and a half to the outside of the International Space Station! Countries monitor our every move. Mosquito breeding grounds are now spied on by satellites equipped with radar altimeters. We're considered pests worldwide. And yet, today, we're the only species guarding the environment by keeping wetlands uninhabitable."

He was angry and passionate. But it wasn't called the 100-Million-Year Lecture for nothing. Aside from Dinnn, half the class was asleep or watching the dandelion seed drift toward the floor.

"Humans have called us awful names for centuries!" Proudnose furiously scribbled on the dusty wall with his nose:

Ugh! (Neanderthal) = *Blood-sucker!*
Muia! (Ancient Greek) = *Blood-sucker!*

Mygga! (Viking) = *Blood-sucker!*
Mogi! (Korean) = *Blood-sucker!*
Sakimês! (Cree) = *Blood-sucker!*
Musket! (American settler) = *Blood-sucker!*
Disease vector! (Modern scientist) = *Blood-sucker!*

His nose drooped with dust. "Other than petty name-calling, humans have yet to focus their attention on us. They generally don't attack unless they sense financial benefits. So we need not worry yet. We have plenty of adversaries, but there is one species more terrible than all others. Hunters so advanced, so highly evolved, so terrifying in flight capability that I dread naming them. We've shared the sky with them for millions of years. In your DNA you all know these creatures. Their ancestor — *Meganeura* — was the largest known flying insect of all time. Our own ancestor *Paleoculicus minutus* (petrified now in a chunk of Cretaceous Canadian amber) tried desperately to evade them. I refer of course to . . . DRAGONFLIES!"

The students who were dozing suddenly sat up.

"Dragonflies were once the size of bald eagles!" Proudnose shouted, his wings outstretched.

He paused and looked around the class.

"Just 300 million years ago, insects grew to enormous sizes due to high oxygen levels in the atmosphere. Dragonflies evolved into the world's supreme flying machines. They now have the best vision in the insect world — seeing in all directions simultaneously with eyes containing 30,000 individual lenses. In flight their legs form basket-shaped traps to catch insects and eat them alive . . ."

Proudnose shook his head mournfully, and his voice trailed off.

"Can we mosquitoes ever defeat such a . . . Renaissance insect?"

He seemed to stare straight at Dinnn.

"No!" he suddenly shouted. "We cannot! All we can do is what we've done through the ages. Know our enemy and avoid them."

As the dandelion seed drifted past him, Proudnose frantically scribbled a drawing on the wall:

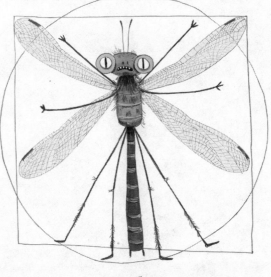

"Behold! The pondhawk dragonfly. The most feared insect predator on the face of the earth."

The class gasped.

"Maybe it's better to be squished against a glass window than to face a painful death in the jaws of one of these monsters. My best advice? If you ever hear the sound of dragonfly wings, fly fast, fly low, and DON'T LOOK BACK!"

The dandelion seed finally floated all the way down to the floor.

Proudnose sighed. "Class is over." He drifted out of the room, his legs dragging on the floor.

Everyone, exhausted by his epic lecture, followed him out the door.

But Dinnn remained alone at the back of the room, motionless, staring at the drawing on the wall.

Parent-Teacher Night

ONE DAY ALL the students took home a leaflet announcing the school's science fair followed by Meet-the-Teacher Night. The homeroom teacher was an old praying mantis with spiky forelegs, and she wasn't friendly. Dinnn's brothers said the evening should be called Meet-the-Creature Night.

Dinnn knew his mother was too busy to go. His dad would have to come.

This was bad news. It could be awkward.

Dinnn's father always dozed off in public. He even fell asleep once in the middle of the crosswalk. Besides, Dinnn hadn't shown up at Study Minute for extra math help, and he was falling behind. His only hope was that Ms. Mantis, with her bad eyesight, wouldn't notice him among his hundreds of older brothers and sisters.

The science fair part of the day, however, was something Dinnn was looking forward to. Students were supposed to raise awareness about different sources of energy, and Dinnn decided to build a little stand across the road from the school.

He worked long into the evening preparing his booth. It took him hours underneath the streetlight, but he managed to bend a blade of grass to the ground and kick sand over its tip to hold it down. It made a perfect table!

He spent the rest of the night collecting droplets of flower nectar, plant juice and root beer from a can in the recycle bin. He spaced them out neatly on the grass blade. The drops looked like a jewel necklace — all laid out so shiny and perfect!

Dinnn was so excited to share his favorite tastes with his classmates, siblings and teachers.

He waited by his booth, ready for his first customer.

But when the sun finally rose, all the mosquitoes flying to school drifted right past Dinnn and his roadside booth. He saw them gather in the willow tree over the school. They set up their own booths in the branches.

No one was on the ground except for Dinnn. And so no one came to his booth.

It was hot by the road. He could see branches swaying in the breeze.

The others likely had a view of the lake, too.

It must be nice up there, he thought.

Soon Dinnn saw all his teachers fly up to inspect the booths high in the tree. He stood still and watched, his legs aching. After an hour or so he sat down on the curb and looked down the empty road.

A few minutes later, he finally saw some mosquitoes coming toward him. He rushed back to his stall and waited.

A group of five females flew down and landed in

front of his booth. Dinnn smiled and gestured toward his display table.

"What you got there, kid?" asked one mosquito. She spoke fast.

"Uh, plant juice and nectar. Root beer, too!"

"Got any red drops?"

"What?"

"Got any *real* juice? The non-vegetarian kind?"

Dinnn pretended to look for blood drops among his display.

"Sorry. I guess I'm out."

"Figures." They all laughed and flew off high into the willow tree.

When the long day finally ended, Dinnn looked down the road one last time.

Not one bug, besides the disinterested females, had visited the table. Not even his brothers and sisters.

Even his teachers had forgotten him.

Dinnn felt his throat burn with a feeling that he was going to cry, but he blinked the tears away. He went back to his grass blade and — suddenly angry at everything — kicked the sand off it. It sprang up and knocked him tumbling into the ditch.

Dinnn crawled back up and brushed himself off. It had not been a good day, so far.

When the time for Meet the Teacher finally came,

Dinnn waited by the ditch for his father. He watched the side of the road, looking for a wobbly speck flying just above the long grass.

Brad Needles, flying slowly as usual, arrived at dusk. When they went into the school, his father floated tiredly through the halls, glancing at student artwork. He kept complaining that there was no place for him to land on the walls.

"Do they expect parents to hover the whole time?" his father said.

Dinnn shrugged.

They arrived at the end of the hall where Ms. Mantis was waiting.

"Mr. Needles. Good evening," she said, tilting her triangular head. "I see little flightless Dinnn is with you."

Dinnn's father smiled. Dinnn tried smiling, too. He glanced around to see if any mosquitoes from his class were on the walls.

His father sat on a dandelion seed in front of Ms. Mantis. He focused his eyes, trying to look alert. On the floor were small drops.

"Would you care for a drop of nectar?" Ms. Mantis asked.

Dinnn's father smiled. "Well, maybe just a drop." He nudged Dinnn. "Son, bring one, please. Hurry."

Dinnn picked one up and walked back slowly, holding the bead between his forelegs so it wouldn't burst.

But by the time he got back, his father was asleep.

Dinnn looked up at Ms. Mantis. She shook her head. They were alone, but there may as well have been a swarm in the room, Dinnn was so embarrassed.

He wished his mom had come. He nudged his father.

"Dad. Wake up!"

His father woke suddenly, kicking for balance.

Dinnn handed his father the drop. His father's eyes widened as he punctured the drop with his long nose and drank.

"Your son's not working to his potential . . ." Ms. Mantis began.

Dinnn's father nodded, still drinking.

"Stillwater School literally has swarms of eager new students coming through our vents each week." She tapped the floor with her spiked leg to get his father's attention. "We can't give your son more time than the others just because he won't lift himself off the ground!"

Dinnn's father sat up. He was trying to listen, but his eyes were unfocused, and he suddenly floated off to the wall to sleep.

"Well, if your father doesn't have the attention span

for a fifteen-second meeting, there's nothing I can do. I've got a busy schedule," Ms. Mantis said, and she left the room.

Dinnn sat there alone and stared at his dad. Then he reached up and tapped his father's back.

"Dad. It's time to go."

His father lifted his head and nodded. He slowly made his way along the wall toward the door. In the hall, mosquitoes of all ages hurried back and forth. They headed outside through vents and gaps in the walls.

"I'm sorry, son. I'm just so tired. With all your brothers and sisters going to school now, that was my 157th parent-teacher interview this week."

"Don't worry about it, Dad," Dinnn said quietly, his shoulders hunched in his jacket.

The Walk Home

DINNN AND HIS father went out the vent and up the ditch to the side of the road.

Dinnn felt tired and cold underneath his leather jacket. The whole way home his dad kept flying into the ditch to sip from roadside flowers for energy. Wind from passing trucks blew him around in the tall grass.

A huge garbage truck rushed past. The wind blew his father's tiny body deep into some raspberry bushes. He flew out again, covered in dust.

"Sometimes I wish I could bite mammals like your mother does. But it's just not my instinct," Dinnn's father said. "I need to find more energy for you kids somehow . . ."

Dinnn climbed over a piece of gravel. "Oh, just forget it."

"What's that?" his dad said.

"Forget it!" Dinnn shouted.

"Forget . . . what?"

"Everything!"

His father stood still now, looking at Dinnn. "What do you mean?"

"No one cares about me or about anything I do!"

His father watched him.

"No one even cares about my jacket."

Dinnn kicked a grain of sand angrily and then walked quickly ahead.

After a minute or so he slowed down. The horizon glowed behind office towers. The dome of sky seemed to hold every little sound Dinnn had known since he was born — insects, seagulls, humming electrical wires, voices.

His father caught up to him. They walked together in silence beside the ditch. Dinnn sensed his father's wing hovering at his back, guiding him off the road.

Under the big fading sky, Dinnn slowly grew less angry. He slowed down, watching the ground. He wasn't mad so much as frustrated, and he couldn't figure out exactly why . . .

"Sorry, Dad."

"It's okay."

They didn't say anything else the rest of the way home. But Dinnn knew his dad cared about him. Even if he was just a skinny mosquito who didn't fly, and the youngest of 401 kids.

The Fall

DINN AMBLED slowly beside the road, daydreaming. It was a hot afternoon, and he was making the long trek home from school.

He looked up and saw a circle of teenage mosquitoes standing in the middle of the road on a manhole cover.

Dinn recognized three of them. The biggest was Dante. He stood surrounded by other members of the Circle. They were tough kids, loafers, a few aimless grads who hung out in ditches near the school.

Dinn walked off the gravel and onto the road. He tried to appear casual, not even glancing over his shoulder to see if a car was coming. He walked more slowly the closer he got to the group, swaggering. His shoulders slouched in his jacket to show its weight.

"Cool jacket..." the big mosquito said when Dinn reached the manhole cover.

A few mosquitoes laughed.

The big mosquito turned. "It is a cool jacket!" He put a foreleg on Dinnn's shoulder.

Dinnn wished his brothers could see him now, hanging out with the cool inner circle of the Circle.

He smiled and looked around.

"Why do you wear that thing?" someone asked.

Dante turned. "It's cool, that's why. The jacket's cool. Right, little brother?"

Dinnn smiled again and nodded. Dante's foreleg tightened around his neck. Dinnn felt crowded by the others, and they pushed him closer to Dante. He felt something under his feet and noticed a silver piece of foil.

"What's that?" Dinnn asked, looking down.

"That's a . . . magic carpet," Dante said, his foot on the foil.

The other mosquitoes laughed.

"Cool," Dinnn said.

"You wanna be in the Circle, kid?"

"Yeah!"

"First you gotta pass a test."

"Okay. What?" Dinnn asked eagerly.

"Take a ride."

"Where?"

"Don't worry. Just stand still. You'll get to use your wings," he said, chuckling.

"Wings?" Dinnn looked up.

Suddenly, Dante didn't have a friendly face. His black compound eyes seemed to stare in all directions at once. He smiled at Dinnn without looking directly at him, as if he hadn't even heard him.

"Just stand on the magic carpet, little brother." Dante nodded his proboscis at the foil.

Dinnn was pulled by his jacket lapels until he stood right on the magic carpet.

"Hold still, now!"

Then Dante took his foot off the foil . . .

The magic carpet immediately levitated, rising up from a draft of air underneath. It tilted to one side. Then the other way.

Dinnn tried to balance, his six legs scrambling. But it was impossible to cling to the slippery foil.

The sheet flew out from under him. A gust lifted him for a second.

Then he fell.

Dinnn fell backwards through the hole in the manhole cover that the foil had hidden. He fell down through the cold empty blackness. He dropped slowly. His jacket, hard and heavy around him, pinned his wings in the silent air.

He fell for five seconds until he splashed into the bottom of the culvert . . . far beneath the road.

Underground

DINN FLOATED on sewage. He looked up at the tiny circle of light in the manhole. It seemed like a distant star.

He heard water. He realized he was in the long tunnel that ran under the road — a place all mosquitoes dreaded.

He scrambled frantically and stood dripping on the mud bank. Ever since the first day of his life when he had almost drowned, Dinn had been terrified of water.

The shallow stream reeked, and the water had a phosphorescent glow.

He looked to the far end of the tunnel. It was completely dark. He heard the sound of water falling there as overflow trickled toward the lake.

He looked the other way and saw faint daylight. It was curtained off by massive spider webs. Dinn knew that beyond those webs was the ditch where teenagers hung out at recess. But not even the coolest mosquitoes in the Circle had ever ventured down here. The webs were too thick and crowded with spiders.

Dinnn's heart was racing.

Looking up at the manhole again, he realized that a flying mosquito could get out quite easily.

But he couldn't fly.

Dinnn clung to the wall and started climbing, but his jacket was soaking wet and twice as heavy as usual. He hadn't climbed more than a few inches before he slipped down.

He tried a few more times, but each time he fell.

The only way to get out of the tunnel was through the huge wall of spider webs that hung between him and the outside.

Dinnn looked at the water. He could see several frog heads just above the surface. They stared blankly in his direction. Beyond them, on the far bank, he noticed a rat asleep in the mud.

Nothing moved.

Dinnn looked back at the looming web. It was a yard away.

Seven spiders watched, motionless. Their legs were tucked underneath their fat bodies. The web swayed slightly in the draft.

Six of the spiders were average sized. The seventh was massive. A wolf spider. Its hairy body rested silently near the water, ready to pounce on anything that moved.

The web stretched across the stream, all the way down to the surface of the water. Dinnn couldn't see a single hole to climb through.

What would my brother in the Wild do? he suddenly wondered.

He dipped his nose in the water. The taste was awful.

Yet he knew that to get past the web, he would have to go in the water.

Dinnn hesitantly lowered himself into the toxic liquid, millimeter by millimeter. Deeper and deeper into slime.

Slowly he inched along, clinging to the mud bank with one leg while treading water with his other five. Only his eyes and nose were out of the water. His hind legs kicked gently.

As Dinnn bobbed past the frogs, a tongue suddenly lashed his back. Luckily his jacket was too slippery to hold on to. He had to keep moving toward the web.

Something like grass brushed against his legs.

"What . . . ?" He glanced down.

The water was alive. Black lines scattered in all directions.

A nest of baby water snakes!

Dinnn turned and saw their mother suddenly rise out of the water. Her pale underbelly gleamed as she lunged at a frog. The entire tunnel exploded with splashing water.

Every creature in the tunnel suddenly sprang to life.

The rat splashed across the water and attacked the snake. To avoid being trampled, Dinnn clung to the mud bank, but the tail of the snake thrashed and knocked him into deeper water.

Dinnn panicked, struggling to get his head up. In the cloudy water he could see the mother snake lashing out at the rat, and the frogs leaping out of her way.

Then, through the surface, he saw the giant wolf spider reach out for him. A long hairy leg stretched over the water to snatch him. When Dinnn rose to breathe, it grabbed him. But a wave washed over them, and the spider lost its grip.

Dinnn kicked desperately toward the web now, trying to evade the spider's long, grasping leg. The spider clambered alongside the water, reaching.

Dinnn screamed.

Suddenly the web was directly above him. It was his only chance. Dinnn took a deep breath and swam down, kicking his six legs as fast as he could. In his

jacket, he sank deeper and deeper. He wriggled and kicked until — somehow — he managed to shed his jacket. His eyes stung and his thorax burned. He was terrified, but he didn't stop kicking until he came out the other side . . .

Free!

❋

Outside, in the day's bright light, Dinnn waded to shore and quickly scrambled up through the crabgrass until he reached the side of the road.

He was covered with mud.

"Holy cow!" someone shouted.

The teens on the road turned and stared at him, amazed.

"The weirdo is still alive!"

Dinnn stared back, exhausted. He was mad.

Dante floated over the road toward Dinnn, glaring back at him.

"How did you . . ."

"You were just pretending to be my friend . . ." Dinnn said, shaking with anger.

"He's a loser, Dante. Let's fly," a voice called.

Dante stared at Dinnn for a second before turning away. Without a word he and the others flew off to the long grass by the road.

Dinnn stood still. Under his feet he could feel the warm cement of the road. With his jacket gone, he felt the weight of mud on his back. The last sun of the day dried the mud on his nose and antennae. His whole body felt like it had an old dry shell around it.

Then he felt something move on his back. A faint, almost forgotten feeling.

His wings stirred.

The Minivan Returns

THE NEXT DAY, Dinnn went on a long walk, exploring vacant lots along the lakefront.

A dozen of his siblings flew past him.

"Where's your jacket?" they called down. But no one stopped to hear his answer.

Dinnn just kept walking. With the weight of his jacket gone, he felt more restless than ever.

Eventually he walked back to the puddle, where his mother was helping her friends watch over new egg rafts. The puddle had been getting smaller over the past few days.

"Where's Dad?" Dinnn asked.

"He was up late watching movies again," she answered irritably.

Dinnn looked off into the distance at the empty parking lot and the big blank movie screen.

He was about to settle in the shade when a huge

car tire rolled in front of him, blocking his way. The car was right above him. He looked up and saw the long dark underside covered in smelly oil and gasoline.

It was as if the sky had gone black.

He walked out from under it and looked up.

It was a red car.

A red minivan. The minivan that had brought his parents to the city! The van from the country, where his half brother lived in the Wild!

He had to tell his mom. He started to run as fast as he could back to the puddle, leaping and hopping.

But his mother was already flying over the hood of the car.

"Dinnn! This way! I know a secret vent we can all go through. Get your brothers and sisters, and your father. We're going to the country!"

"Okay!"

In his excitement, Dinnn turned and stepped on a pile of melted bubblegum. His six feet sank in the warm pink muck.

"Hurry, Dinnn!"

Dinnn was stuck. He struggled and pulled and squirmed. He couldn't miss this chance to see the Wild.

He started to beat his wings.

He yanked a foot free. Then another. Then another.

His wings beat faster and faster, and the next thing he knew . . .

He was in the air!

He was in the air. And he was *flying*!

Dinnn floated in an uneven spiral up to the car and drifted into a vent, following the sound of his mother's voice. Soon all four hundred siblings flew in after him, one by one, through a small vent in the dashboard.

Finally their father came tumbling through, too.

"Okay, kids. Spread out!" he said, panting. "We're going to the Wild!"

Dinnn's brothers and sisters floated over and patted him on the back.

"Well flown, Dinnn!" his dad and mom both said, hugging him.

"Well, it's a start . . ." Dinnn said. "I'm still a bit shaky."

Then he joined his siblings buzzing against the windows. They rode the gusts from the air vents, tumbling and tapping and turning along the glass with joy.

Dinnn was the happiest he had ever been. When he looked at his mother, he thought he could see tears in her eyes. She was resting on the front window, staring ahead as if ready to blast off into the sky.

He knew she was thinking about her son in the country, and the rest of her family there.

As the engine started, Dinnn saw his dad reach out to hold her foreleg. The car began to move.

On the Highway

THE LAKESIDE Drive-In disappeared in the distance, barely the size of a matchbox. Dinnn and the others gathered on the rear window and watched in amazement as the big white screen got smaller and smaller.

Moments later the minivan was rushing along the highway. Dinnn was hypnotized by the view. He watched the fields rush by. Rolling hills, islands of trees, occasional farm houses — even cows.

Dinnn had never moved so fast.

Thousands of seconds rushed by — 7,199, to be precise.

❋

Soon it was dusk. And dusk, to any mosquito, is the most magical time of the day.

They slowed down and pulled into a gas station along the side of the highway.

"Well, I'll be . . ." Dinnn's father said, bouncing against the glass. "This is the gas station, honey! Kids! This is my gas station! This is where your mother and I met!"

The next thing Dinnn knew, his brothers and sisters were flying up into the evening air, following their dad to a big neon sign in bright blue letters.

Dinnn floated out, awkwardly at first, until he

gained a little altitude and caught a draft of warm air lifting him up.

It was just as beautiful as his dad had described. High up above the car, the letters seemed to be touching the stars . . .

GAS FOR SALE!

Old Friends

A SWARM of mosquitoes gathered around them, and Dinnn could hear a thousand voices yelling all at once.

"Brad! Brad!"

"Brad the Needle's back in town!"

Within minutes, Dinnn's father had introduced 927 of his friends. They buzzed happily around the blue glow. It was beautiful. Dinnn felt at home in this new place, where the air was cool and clear, and the land was wide and dark under the stars.

Then the minivan's engine roared.

Dinnn's mother suddenly called out, "Kids! Back to the car."

They all nose-dived toward the minivan. Their father was swarmed.

"Stay with us, Brad!" the floaters called.

Their mother dragged their father by his leg. She

got him to the car and pushed him in the window. Then, as she was trying to follow him . . .

The window closed.

Dinn's mother frantically tapped the window with her nose, but the car was pulling away.

She yelled through the glass, "Go on, children. I'll be all right. The car comes back this way. I'll wait here . . ."

She flew as fast as she could alongside the minivan.

"Brad, look after the kids . . ."

At the rear window she shouted, "Watch out for dragonf — "

Dinn watched his mother's shape get smaller and smaller.

Soon there was only darkness beside the highway. Darkness and dark trees and the light of the moon.

PART 2
In the Wild

Lost

THE MINIVAN pulled off the highway onto a bumpy dirt road. The headlights shone on trees, and the car rocked around on the rutted narrow path, driving past bushes and tall grass.

Finally it came to a full stop underneath a huge pine tree.

One of the car doors opened.

In the darkness, all Dinnn heard was . . .

. . . *crickets crickets. . .*

Slowly, out of the wild woods, he heard a voice. Then more voices.

It was like a waterfall of voices.

Mosquito voices! Mosquitoes were coming from everywhere.

Soon they were surrounded by noisy mosquito relatives, all of whom looked like their mother.

"Where's Corrina?"

"I don't see her . . ."

"Check the rear window! That's where we saw her last . . ."

Suddenly, the swarm of mosquitoes parted like smoke. A tiny ancient-looking mosquito floated through them. She was an old grandmother mosquito. A gray, bristly little thing, her wings were dry and thin.

But her eyes were bright, and damp with tears. She perched delicately on the rearview mirror.

"You children look so much like your mother," her voice wavered.

A few country mosquitoes laughed.

The old mosquito floated over and hugged Dinnn, ruffling his antennae with her nose. Then she did the same to all of his four hundred siblings.

Before long, hundreds more mosquitoes were hovering near them, drifting with them in the air as they floated past a tire swing toward the dark pine tree.

"What are your names?"

"How come your mom's not with you . . .?"

Before Dinnn knew what was happening, they were all swept up in a swarm, high into a pine tree and through a dark knothole.

Gus

EVERYONE was quiet for a few seconds. All the city relatives and country relatives looked at each other.

Their father's buzz broke the silence. He introduced himself and told the story of how he had first met Corrina at the gas station, and how he had just lost her tonight.

Then, exhausted by the long day, he collapsed. Four country mosquitoes carried him to a pool of water in the knothole and let him float with his skinny legs sticking up in the air. His nose bobbed as he snored.

"Poor fellow," the old grandmother mosquito said. "Let him sleep. He looks like a floater, and life can be hard for floaters."

"Well, it looks like *I* gotta take care of ya," someone said. A voice was coming from outside the tree.

Dinnn and his brothers and sisters peered from the knothole. They stared into the darkness below. A huge mosquito rose slowly out of the dark, floating up from the tire swing.

He was enormous and hairy, with a deep buzzing sound. He flew smoothly into the knothole, drifting calm as a hawk. He was the coolest-looking mosquito Dinnn had ever seen.

"You guys ever been to the Big Wild before?" the mosquito asked.

They all shook their heads.

Their father sneezed, his wings sputtering in the pool.

"My name's Gus," the huge mosquito said. "I hear your ma didn't make it."

Dinnn and his siblings nodded and looked down sadly at the moon's reflection in the pool. It shook slightly in the water, stirred by their father.

"I don't have parents, myself," Gus said, looking away. "My dad left when I was born. They say pondhawks wiped out my brothers and sisters. My mom left the woods soon after." He pointed toward the dark forest below. "With your dad being a floater and all, the grown-ups say I've got to keep you safe. First lesson: anyone here know what a pondhawk dragonfly is?"

Dinnn's wings began to buzz. He couldn't believe his luck.

"I know!" he blurted. He half-flew over the water, splashing across the pool and tripping over his father's nose. He stood in front of Gus, dripping.

"Who are you?" Gus said, looking down at Dinnn.

"I'm Dinnn. With three Ns. I know everything about dragonflies. They have unbelievable flying powers. They have four wings and they all move independently, so dragonflies can go up, down, backwards, sideways, or turn instantly. They're perfect flying machines. Large ones fly over thirty miles an hour! There are hundreds of kinds of dragonflies and each kind hunts differently! They're like flying sharks. Hawkers like to zigzag in open air. Gleaners like to float slowly through dense vegetation. Dragonflies see in color and have the best vision in the whole insect world. They can see more colors than humans, even into the ultra-violet range . . ."

Dinnn's brothers and sisters all stared at their little brother, amazed.

"They live all over the world. Four species of giant dragonflies live in Australia's swamplands alone. In this part of the wild there's dozens of species: the Swift River cruiser, the swamp spreadwing, the seepage dancer, the arrowhead spiketail, the painted skimmer, the riffle snaketail . . . and the pondhawk, I bet! I bet big pondhawks are very common hereabouts . . ." Dinnn suddenly stopped talking. He swallowed and looked outside at the dark forest.

"Some say pondhawks are the most ferocious of all dragonflies."

Gus hovered above Dinnn. The air from his big wings made Dinnn's eyes water, and he blinked.

"Impressive stuff, Darwin," he said.

"Dinnn," Dinnn said quietly.

"Have you ever seen a dragonfly, Dinnn?"

"No." Dinnn glanced around.

"Look, I don't know what they taught you in city schools but . . ."

"In Stillwater School we learned lots!" Dinnn said. "We mosquitoes are pretty cool, too. We can smell human breath from one hundred feet away! Mr. Bluebottle said mosquitoes fly up to four hours nonstop and can travel up to ten miles a night, at a speed of two miles per hour! And when it's dark we can even navigate by the moon and stars. Our wings beat up to six hundred times a second. That's why we make a buzzing sound — "

Gus floated forward.

"Listen," he said. "You and all the rest of you city mosquitoes . . . just follow me tonight, okay? And stick close."

Harvest Moon

GUS WAS already buzzing at flight speed. He turned and faced Dinnn and his siblings, counting them with his long nose.

"One, two, three, four, five, six . . . Hold still! How many are you?" he shouted.

"Four hundred," Dinnn's oldest brother said.

"Four hundred and one," Dinnn shouted from behind his siblings.

"Look," Gus said. "There's a thirty-foot drop from here to the forest floor. The safest way to fly out of these pine branches is to float down through them slowly . . . then level out at about six feet."

Gus leapt and floated off into the dark.

"Stay away from the house," he shouted. "They just sprayed it with insecticide. And don't hang out by the door. The porch light is a bug zapper."

Those were the last words he said before he dove

down through the pine branches at a speed that left Dinnn and his siblings far behind.

They followed Gus down through the thick branches. Dinnn flew slowly, bumping into pine needles, until he finally reached the bottom branch of the tree. Gus and the others were already waiting, hovering at the end of the branch.

"Took ya long enough," one of his brothers said.

"Sorry," Dinnn said, landing awkwardly on a pine cone.

"Okay, we're all here," Gus said. "Follow me."

Gus flew past the windows of the cottage, into the woods and down a long hill. The others flew as fast as they could, with Dinnn far behind them all. He could barely see the mosquito ahead of him, and he struggled to keep up, dodging branches and leaves to keep his siblings in sight. His wings were aching.

They flew deep into the woods, and it grew darker and darker. Dinnn grew more and more scared. He realized he wouldn't have been able to do any of this if he still had his jacket. For a moment, flying through the forest, with the wind against his leg bristles, he felt freer than he'd ever felt in his life.

Dinnn shouted out in a happy voice to one of his sisters flying ahead of him, "This is *great!*"

"Shut up and just hurry!" she shouted back over her shoulder.

Flying at over one mile per hour, they finally broke through a blackberry bush and came into a clearing. The ground was covered in ferns and long grass. Trees grew beside a huge pond, and the water was still and reflected the moon.

They flew along the pond's shore. And there above them, among the trees and bushes, sparkling green lights flashed on and off.

Fireflies!

Fireflies floated everywhere. Sometimes they came so close that Dinnn could see their faces. One firefly nodded at him as it passed.

They were beautiful — the most magical things Dinnn had ever seen.

"What is this place?"

"Odonata Pond," Gus said. "We come here at night, especially when the city people are out swimming."

There was a dock by the water. Dinnn landed and walked over to a diving board. He walked to the end of it and for fun jumped up, hovering above the water . . .

"*Don't!*" Gus shouted.

As he shouted, a huge fish — a largemouth bass — leapt out of the water. Its enormous mouth grazed

Dinnn's hind leg before it fell back, splashing into the lake.

Dinnn fell onto the dock and ran to the shore.

"You gotta watch out!" Gus said, hovering over Dinnn. "Never go over the water unless you absolutely have to. A fish will eat you if you fly that low, especially at this hour."

Gus counted everyone again, making sure they were all there.

"Just be careful. This is a dangerous place. By morning an army of gliders and hawkers will be coasting along the shoreline looking for us."

Then he turned to them and relaxed a little and smiled.

"But at night," he said, "this place is pretty much ours."

Crouching Mosquito,
Hidden Dragonfly

GUS TURNED his back to the pond and flew low into the marsh. They drifted silently into the long grass. Dinnn floated right at Gus's elbow. He could tell it bothered Gus, but he did it anyway.

They were flying so slowly that Dinnn could hear a frog blink and a minnow turn in the water.

"Where are we going?" he asked loudly.

"Shhh!" Gus said. "We're entering a resting spot."

"Whose resting spot?" Dinnn whispered, looking down nervously.

"Dragonflies," Gus whispered. "They sleep here at night. They hang on cattails."

Terrified, Dinnn looked around in the darkness.

"There." Gus stopped and pointed. "Right behind you."

Dinnn hovered by a bulrush. The tall reed towered above him.

He couldn't see anything at first. But as his eyes adjusted in the moonlight, he suddenly saw . . .

Two huge dragonflies. They were massive, clearly from the pondhawk clan. But they were fast asleep, hanging there like silent chainsaws.

Dinnn was so startled, he dropped to the ground and started to run. He didn't look back. Then he remembered he could fly, and he buzzed his wings and rose up the hill and into the woods. He flew so fast that even Gus didn't catch him at first. But halfway to the pine tree, Gus reached over and stuck his nose into Dinnn's fluttering wings, and Dinnn sputtered and tumbled to the ground.

He was breathing so fast he couldn't talk. When his brothers and sisters and Gus found him, they dusted him off and helped him float into the air again.

Gus was at his side, and he elbowed Dinnn good-naturedly.

"I thought you knew dragonflies don't hunt at night. Being an expert and all."

"Yeah. I forgot." Dinnn tried to look cool. "But I've only seen them in . . . movies."

"Well, you've seen them in *real* life now."

On the way back to the pine tree, they passed a

garden and an overflowing compost bin beside the cabin.

Gus paused to sip nectar from a sunflower.

"Here, have a drink, Dinnn. You look tired."

Dinnn drifted over, checking the stem for dragon-flies. Then he landed and buried his nose in the sunflower.

His brothers sipped from the sunflower, too.

Dinnn's sisters landed nearby, on a raccoon. It had opened the bin and was rummaging in the compost. The raccoon didn't seem to feel their little bites.

As they flew off again, they passed the cabin window. Light and music poured out. There was laughter, too.

Dinnn didn't feel like stopping and staring through the screen window with the others, so he drifted alone up to the knothole in the big pine tree. He dropped to the floor, exhausted, and fell into a deep sleep.

Dinnn was too tired to hear his father snoring in the pool. He was too tired even to dream.

Ride the Wild Drop

DINN WOKE up with sunlight on his face.

A beam of light warmed his wings. He fluttered them a little. His tiny back muscles were sore. They ached from his flight the previous night.

His brothers and sisters were waking up, too. But Gus was nowhere to be seen. A few dozen country relatives floated around, sipping tree sap.

Dinn's father woke and stood by the pool.

"You know, son," he said, stretching. "This clean country air knocks me out. So much pure oxygen. Not like city air. I can see why your mother loved the country."

He paused, looking thoughtfully out the knothole. "I wonder how she's doing at the old gas station . . ."

Just then Gus buzzed into the knothole.

"Yikes!" Dinn's father said, stumbling backwards into the pool. "You spooked me, big fella! Whew! You fly fast!"

"Sorry, Mr. Needles," Gus said. "Okay, everyone. Drink up. We're gonna have fun today!"

Dinnn and his siblings drank their tree sap. Pretty soon all four hundred and two young mosquitoes were flying out the knothole into the bright sun.

They flew in and out of the shade all day. Gus told them to stay close to the pine tree, and so they played within the giant branches. They tumbled over one another in the cool air, laughing and playing hide-and-seek behind the pine cones.

When it got windy, Dinnn clung to the tree. He knew mosquitoes could be blown away by a wind moving faster than they could fly.

In the late afternoon it rained. Gus was impatient and bored waiting for the rain to stop. He decided to teach them how to dodge raindrops.

"Watch and learn," he said.

He stood on the tip of a branch. He lifted his wings and was about to leap into the open air when a creaky voice called out, "Gus! You be careful."

It was their grandmother. The old mosquito coughed and cleared her throat.

"Remember what happened to your grandpa here?" She nudged an old mosquito leaning beside her. "He separated his shoulder flying in a rainstorm!"

"Yeah, I remember. So?" Gus said.

"So, he was a showoff just like you. Then a stray raindrop caught him and knocked him senseless. Now he flies like he's drunk four times his bodyweight."

"I'm quicker than him, Grandma!" Gus called back.

She shook her head.

Gus suddenly flew out beyond the cover of the tree. He flew brilliantly in a zigzag, dodging hundreds of raindrops expertly. He made it to a nearby tree and landed. Then he turned around and waved.

Dinnn and his siblings and all the local mosquitoes cheered.

After catching his breath, Gus flew back toward them — in a straight line!

He was almost all the way to the tree branch when . . .

A raindrop hit him.

Gus suddenly plummeted downward.

The raindrop surrounded him. Gus twirled around inside the drop! And in that instant he appeared to lose any sense of up, down, left or right. Gus had to "ride the drop" and stay calm . . .

And somehow get out before he hit the ground.

Then — just as suddenly — Gus broke through the raindrop's other side. He was soaking wet and wobbly from the sudden acceleration, but he was okay. He flew up and landed safely on the same branch he'd started from.

Gus shook the rain off his wings.

"Whew!" he said, shaken.

For some reason, Dinnn wished his mother was with them. If only she could be here now watching Gus, too.

Chariots on Fire

BY LATE AFTERNOON the rain had stopped. Gus took all of them up what he called the Staircase — the highest branches of the tree.

He pointed in the distance to the west. Odonata Pond sparkled gold in the setting sun.

"Look!" Gus shouted.

Dinnn looked, squinting as hard as he could.

Suddenly he saw it move. A giant Ferris wheel rising out of the trees on the far shore. Fiery red lights glittered in the sky and reflected on the water.

"Wow! What is that?"

"They call it the Chariots on Fire. It comes here every summer for the jamboree."

"Let's go!" they all said.

"It's a long flight. It'll take a half hour to fly there at top speed. One of you go ask your dad."

Dinnn's oldest brother plunged through the tree

branches. He flew back up a minute later.

"Dad's asleep. The other grown-ups say it's okay, but we have to be back before the sun comes up."

"Great. Let's rock!" said Gus.

They were about to take off when Dinn felt someone's wing on his shoulder. He turned and saw his grandmother.

"Now listen, little Dinnn," she said. "You don't have to go. You could stay here with me tonight. We could knit and watch the fireflies."

His grandmother looked at him tenderly. Hundreds of fireflies were already blinking their green lights along the shore of Odonata Pond.

Dinnn thought about his life back in the city. Walking along the road in his black jacket. The ladybug crossing guard. His teachers. His dad snoring in the puddle in the parking lot. The dull afternoons at the car wash. The dragonfly nightmares.

He looked up and saw stars and the bright moon glowing more brightly than he'd ever seen it before.

He made up his mind.

But just as he was about to shout, "I have to go!" his grandmother shoved him off the tree.

Suddenly he was flying under the moon across the treetops, flying as fast as he could behind a cloud of 478 other mosquitoes.

They were all heading toward the giant Ferris wheel!

❋

After half an hour Dinnn could hear music and people's voices below. He heard screams and the sound of huge generators and engines as the rides came to life in the night.

All the music and sounds and smells of popcorn and hotdogs made him feel dizzy.

"Where do we land?" someone shouted.

They were over the fairgrounds now, and Dinnn's wings were numb from the effort of flying so far.

"Land by the ticket booth with all the lights on it," Gus said. "Beside the candyfloss machine. We can rest a bit there before heading to the Chariots on Fire."

He dived down toward the ticket booth, and the rest followed close behind. Soon all 479 mosquitoes were perched on a wire lined with little red jalapeño pepper-shaped lightbulbs.

Gus shouted, "Remember, the dragonflies wake at dawn. Keep an eye out for sunrise."

Dinnn drifted closer to Gus. He knew one thing for sure. He did not want to be left behind.

❋

The whole cloud of mosquitoes rose up into the night air and flew toward the Ferris wheel. The spinning wheel was full of people laughing and screaming as they rose up, riding in screened-in cages that swung wildly like porch swings one hundred feet in the air.

Dinnn stayed right under Gus's nose everywhere he went. He could barely keep up. They flew to the top of the wheel and hovered there, watching it spin.

"Wait here," Gus said.

The big wheel finally slowed. The highest cage was swinging in the moonlight. Three rowdy human teenagers rocked the cage back and forth while the giant machine loaded passengers below.

"Follow me," Gus said. He dived down through the screen and into the cage. Dinnn and the others followed. Some of his female cousins bit the people, who were too distracted with excitement and noise and laughter to bother swatting them. The mosquitoes buzzed freely in and out of their hair.

Dinnn clung to a metal pole. Soon the wheel's engine rattled to life, and the cage dropped in a terrifying plunge to the ground.

It was like the day Dinnn was born. His thorax rose up into his throat and his six legs buckled as he clutched the cold metal pole and tried to hang on. The wind rushed with such force that he felt as if his wings would tear off. He pressed them against his sides.

Each spin of the wheel lasted a life cycle. The wheel would stop and then start, over and over. It was a circle of life for sure! Gus and the others floated in the air, half-falling, half-flying.

Everyone was deliriously happy.

Everyone except Dinnn. He was terrified.

Whenever the wheel stopped, the country mosquitoes flew to the floor and sipped the sticky puddles of spilled cola, and the females hovered and bit new riders who entered the cage.

It was a magical world for a mosquito. They had everything they needed, and the ride seemed to go on forever. Up and down, up and down, around and around. Under the moon and stars in the swirling lights and loud music and electricity of the jamboree.

Suddenly the wheel stopped. The lights in the fairground went out one by one.

The cage was empty now, and it rocked back and forth in the wind.

A storm was coming. In the growing wind a mosquito could get hurt, blown across the sky into another county.

"What do we do now?" Dinnn asked as he crouched to avoid a gust of wind.

"Don't exactly know," Gus said, sounding unsure of himself for the first time. He was looking at the horizon.

The sky in the east had a faint light in it. A yellow line was glowing.

Dawn was coming.

Enter the Dragonfly

"WE'VE GOT to fly now!" Gus shouted. "It's now or never, everyone. We've got to go!"

They all agreed. Even though the wind was outrageously strong, it was better to fly now than try to cross Odonata Pond at dawn when hundreds of dragonflies would start to patrol the territory.

Four hundred and seventy-seven mosquitoes immediately poured out of the cage in a long cloud, flying toward the lake, buzzing across the open water.

But two mosquitoes were still in the empty cage of the Ferris wheel: Gus and Dinnn.

Dinnn couldn't move.

"I know you're scared," Gus said. "I am, too. But you've got to let go of that pole." He held out his wing, hovering above Dinnn.

Dinnn shook his head. His eyes were wide and staring in all directions. He saw trees bending in the wind.

He glanced down.

"Can't we just walk around the lake?" he asked.

"No way. It would take weeks."

Dinnn shivered with fear, but with all his willpower he peeled a front leg from the pole.

Finally, he held it out, shaking, to Gus. Dinnn's other five legs were still clinging to the pole.

"Concentrate!" Gus said.

Dinnn managed to loosen two more legs, but three legs still clasped the pole.

He looked at Gus. Gus had stayed behind to save him. He was like a brother. One who cared for him. Dinnn didn't want to let him down.

Then Gus looked up and yelled, "Dragonflies!"

Dinnn turned — and Gus pulled him off the pole, through the wire mesh and into the air.

They flew hard against the wind.

As Gus flew alongside Dinnn, he shouted, "I said that to get you to let go. There are no dragonflies, but we've got to get out of here."

Pondhawks!

GUS AND DINNN flew across the water. They had to fly low to avoid gusts of wind. Staying in a straight line was impossible. Once Dinnn stalled against the wind and sank in the air. Gus caught him and guided him back up before he hit the water.

When they were halfway across the pond, a yellow beam of light suddenly lit up the water. The sun rose above the trees. Dinnn saw his cousins and brothers and sisters a hundred feet away, waiting for them on the shore amid the bulrushes.

"Fly faster! Faster!" they shouted.

Then, above the sound of his cousins' and siblings' voices, Dinnn heard a terrible noise.

It was a noise he'd only heard once before, and in his nightmares. The unmistakable thumping sound of . . .

Dragonfly wings.

Gus shouted, "Fly down, Dinnn! Go down and zig-zag!"

Dinnn's eyes were bugging out of his head. He felt like his body was on fire. When he looked over his shoulder he saw Gus flying above him — and two giant blue pondhawk dragonflies racing toward him.

They were flying faster than anything Dinnn had ever seen fly.

They flew faster than birds.

Dinnn dove toward the water just as one pondhawk veered to follow him.

Near the shore, in some bulrushes, something silvery glinted in the sun. Dinnn turned and flew straight toward it.

The pondhawk's giant wings were crackling like electric wires. Dinnn could almost feel their wind on his back.

He felt he should fly to the exact spot of the silvery thing. If he could just reach it . . .

Dinnn led the dragonfly into the outcrop of cattails toward the almost invisible silvery thread.

Just as he was about to fly into it, he ducked.

And the pondhawk flew straight into the spider web, suddenly caught there, struggling.

The cousins and siblings on shore gasped . . .

"Did you see that?!"

"Way to go, Dinnn!"

Dinnn rose up in the air again and spun around. His wings were going unbelievably fast, beating over five hundred times a second.

"Help!" Gus shouted.

Dinnn turned and saw Gus flying toward him. The other pondhawk — even larger than the first — crisscrossed in the air right behind him. Then it flew above Gus.

Forgetting how afraid he was, Dinnn flew toward Gus.

"Follow me!" Dinnn shouted. Gus followed him, and so did the pondhawk.

Dinnn had a gut feeling he should get as close to the water as possible. He flew in a desperate zigzag, like Gus had shown him. The dragonfly was toying with them, moving ten times faster, turning, diving, circling. Dinnn let it build up speed and saw it zoom right overhead as if he was standing still. He flew straight toward the dock.

"Hurry! Hurry!" all the cousins and siblings screamed on the shore.

The dragonfly turned back one more time and rose up high into the air. Then it dived down in a final swoop . . .

The diving board was just a few feet away from

Dinnn and Gus. The dragonfly was right behind them. And as they reached the board, Dinnn turned in mid-air and grasped Gus around the wings, pulling him . . .

All of a sudden, a giant fish jumped out of the water. In midleap it swallowed the dragonfly whole!

Dinnn and Gus fell — bounced off the board — and splashed into the water. They sputtered and climbed up on a leaf and, using their noses, paddled to shore.

They arrived on the mud bank to the sound of cheering and celebrating of every mosquito in the county.

PART 3
The Return

Home

When Dinnn finally woke up, it was early afternoon. He moved slowly, still groggy from his long and wild night. He looked around and saw the other mosquitoes lying on their backs. Some of them had bits of cotton candy and chocolate stuck to their wings. Others were slowly trying to stand, shielding their eyes from the sunlight streaming through the knothole.

Dinnn heard a car door slam. He looked out and saw the red minivan parked near the tire swing.

The cabin people were packing up and putting things in the trunk.

Dinnn didn't want to go home yet. He floated outside the knothole and looked around.

"Gus?" he called.

No one answered.

Dinnn flew to the tire swing and looked inside.

Aside from some stagnant water, it was empty. He flew back up to the tree.

"Where's Gus?" he asked.

"He'll be here to say goodbye," his grandmother said, helping the old grandfather put on his sweater.

Suddenly Dinn's father flew by holding a tiny flower.

"Time to go, kids!" he shouted. "Mom's been buzzing around a gas station for days. Hopefully this buttercup will make it up to her! Did you know that if you put it under your chin, your chin glows?"

One by one, all the country mosquito relatives drifted through the shade to say goodbye. Dinn looked at his grandmother perched on the rearview mirror. Her eyes were full of tears. Her nose trembled as she spoke.

"We'll miss you kids . . ."

Dinn flew up to the top of the tree and called Gus's name as loud as he could.

There was still no answer.

"Dinn, hurry!" his father called, hovering by an open window.

Dinn flew down and floated to the back of the car where his brothers and sisters were waving to hundreds of relatives.

"Bye, Grandma. Bye, everybody!"

"Goodbye, children! Come visit again!"

Dinnn looked quietly out the window and wondered if he'd ever see Gus again.

❋

They drove slowly down the country lane. Dinnn watched as the tall pine tree got smaller and smaller. Soon they were on the highway, moving fast, speeding toward the gas station where their mother had been left behind.

Finally they saw a sign:

GAS FOR SALE!

As they drove into the station, Dinnn's father stood on the dashboard holding his tiny buttercup. Dinnn could tell by the nervous way his dad peered through the windshield that he was probably going to get the cold shoulder-wing.

Sure enough, his mother buzzed right past his dad and the flower. But she was excited to see the kids. She hugged all 401 of them again and again.

When a gas-station attendant came to the car, fifty-seven floater friends gathered by the driver's window, hoping to hitch rides to the city. But Dinnn's father quickly waved them away.

"Guys, seriously. It's not a good time. Try some other car!" he shouted through the window.

On the highway again, Dinnn's mother asked each of the kids about their time in the country. Dinnn told her all about Gus, and about escaping the dragonflies. She turned and stared out the window, as if daydreaming.

Suddenly she turned back.

"What's that sound?"

"What's what sound?"

"I hear singing from the front of the car. Doesn't anyone else hear it?"

"I don't hear anything, Mom," Dinnn said.

"Someone is singing," she said. "Is the radio on?"

Dinnn's dad floated over the stereo speakers. "Nope. I don't hear anything. Shall I turn it on for you?" He tried hard to press the radio buttons, hoping to please her. "Perhaps I'll sing . . .?"

"No," she said, and looked out the window.

Dinnn watched his mother. He thought of all the things she'd missed during the past few days. From the way she rested her forehead on the window, he knew she was sad.

She was sad because she never got to see her lost son, her son in the country.

❊

They arrived home in the parking lot of the Lakeside Drive-In Theater just before sunset.

Dinnn, the last one out of the car, floated slowly down to the gravel. When he touched down, his home felt different. It felt as if he'd been away for ages.

At the edge of the parking lot, a group of teenagers stood near the ditch. Dinnn saw Dante and a few others. They looked at him and snickered, but Dinnn didn't care.

He left the parking lot and drifted along the road.

He saw a mosquito sitting on the curb by the bus shelter. It was a small mosquito, a kid a few weeks younger than him.

The young mosquito squinted and glanced up at Dinnn.

All of a sudden Dinnn noticed what the kid was wearing. His black jacket!

He sat beside the mosquito.

"Hi, there, kid . . ." Dinnn said.

"Hey," the mosquito answered casually.

"Where'd you get that cool jacket?"

"In the ditch. A few days back."

"You know, I think it belonged to me . . ."

The young mosquito shrugged. "Finders keepers."

"I didn't mean — "

"You snooze, you lose."

"You can keep it. No problem."

They sat on the curb together in silence.

"I wonder . . ." Dinnn began. "Can you fly in it? When I wore it I couldn't fly."

"I don't need to fly."

"Why do you wear it?"

"Because it's cool," the little mosquito paused, then added, ". . . man."

"Don't you want to fly someday?"

The mosquito kid shrugged. He stared at the sunset.

Then he pointed. "What's that?"

They saw a large dark shape walking down the middle of the road. The shape got bigger. It was a huge mosquito, and it seemed to be carrying something on its shoulder.

Then it called out, "Hey, Dinnn!"

Gus! Gus was in the city!

Gus walked up to the curb. He was covered in oil and grease, his wings slick with black greasy muck. On his shoulder sat a little firefly, also greasy.

"What happened?" Dinnn asked, amazed. "How did you get here?"

Gus sat down in front of Dinnn and the young mosquito. The firefly slumped over.

"Well," Gus said, "I got up early to find a goodbye

gift for your family. As I passed the car I heard crying and found a firefly stuck in the radiator. He was lost and alone and had no family. So I helped him out. But somehow we got trapped under the hood. When the car started, we fell onto the oil pan. And we rode the whole trip like that. It was so scary, I sang the whole way!"

He smiled at the firefly. "Isn't that right, little buddy?"

"Yeah," the firefly said dully. "I never wanna hear 'Raindrops Keep Fallin' on My Head' again."

"When I was little my mom sang it to me all the time . . ." Gus said.

Then Dinnn heard someone buzz toward them.

"Excuse me, what did you say?"

It was his mother, Corrina. She floated over the road and looked at Gus closely.

"He said his mom used to sing 'Raindrops Keep Fallin' on My Head,'" the firefly said, staring at the ground and shaking his head.

Corrina stared at Gus. Her eyes looked hazy.

"Gus, this is Mom," Dinnn said. "Mom, this is Gus. He's been like a big brother to me."

The country mosquito quickly wiped the grease off the firefly and offered it to Corrina.

"Dinnn's a brave little guy," Gus said. "A real hero."

Dinnn's mother thanked Gus. Then she hugged him. Her eyes were happy and full of tears.

As she hugged him, the firefly got stuck between them and began to glow.

In the distance, fireworks flew up and burst brightly in the darkening sky.

Finally she said, "I missed you . . . every day."

Gus didn't know what to say.

She hugged Gus tighter — her long-lost child. She had so much to tell him . . . so much to ask. But the firefly kept squirming, and finally it slipped into the evening sky and blinked as it floated over the parking lot toward the drive-in.

"Wow, cool firefly!" the little mosquito said, getting up off the curb.

He took off his jacket and floated higher to see.

THE END

Author's Note

FROM THE TIME I was five years old, my older brothers and sisters and I lived in an old farmhouse each summer, where we grew up with mosquitoes. There were a lot of ripped screen windows. Mosquitoes snuck in and drifted silent as dust along the wall. At night they floated up staircases or grates in the floor and hovered in the dark. If you switched the light on they would blend into the old wallpaper. They seemed to have personalities, which they hid just by holding still. When the light went out, a tiny battle horn sounded, and an invisible army charged across the air. It may as well have been the thunder of hooves on a drawbridge.

This story tries to walk a millimeter in one quiet and lonesome mosquito's shoes. Some physical feats in the book aren't possible — I'm pretty sure mosquitoes can't bite through whale blubber — but I have tried to include much factual information as well. There are many things to learn about mosquitoes — from their ability to smell human breath in darkness from 100 feet away, to the way they navigate by the moon and stars, or survive a direct hit from a raindrop.

The following books were helpful resources: *Dragonflies and Damselflies of the East* by Dennis Paulson, *Mosquito* by Richard Jones, and *Bugs Britannica* by Peter Marren and Richard Mabey. Parts of Proudnose's lecture drew sips of energy from articles such as "Mosquito Survives in Outer Space"

(Alexander Peslyak, *RIA Novosti*), "Hunting Mosquitoes from Space" (Jonathan Amos, *BBC*), "Giant Bugs Eaten Out of Existence by First Birds?" (Ker Than, *National Geographic News*), and "How Mosquitoes Survive Collisions with Raindrops" (Eric R. Olson, *Scientific American*). The song "Raindrops Keep Fallin' on My Head" was sung originally by B.J. Thomas and written by Hal David and Burt Bacharach. Dinnn's name was inspired by Elston Gunnn, a little-known piano player who drifted onto the music scene in the Midwest in 1959. The epigraph is a line from the song "No, Doctor, No" by the great calypsonian The Mighty Sparrow.

Acknowledgments

THANK YOU first to my daughter, for asking if mosquitoes have to wear jackets when it's cold. Dinnn's story began because of her. Lilla, Akash and Calin, I love you very much.

Love to Sang-Mi. Thanks for giving so much help, and for patience when discussing the inner lives of mosquitoes.

I want to thank Groundwood's great publisher, Sheila Barry, for letting a manuscript with a mosquito protagonist land on her desk. I'm especially grateful to Patsy Aldana — a wonderfully generous and gifted editor — for believing in a small story from the beginning, and for her care guiding its flight. Many thanks to Shelley Tanaka for amazing insights and great help with the manuscript. Gracias to Erica Salcedo for creating humorous and beautiful drawings. Thanks to Groundwood's brilliant designer, Michael Solomon. And to Nan Froman, Suzanne Sutherland, Gillian Fizet, Barbara Howson, Cindy Ma and Fred Horler.

To Dad and to Mom — love always, and thanks. To Steve, Sky, Tory, North, Quint, Esta and Kristin. To all my cousins, aunts and uncles. And nephews and nieces — Khyber, Galen, Quincy, Mackenzie, Zachary, Tara, Sasha, Dillon, Corbin, Gemma, Finnegan and Graley.

Growing up I had a best friend, Christopher, who was the truest friend to follow in the wilderness of youth. His grandmother's farm was by a long lake, and we would drift over unknown worlds in a small boat, fishing all day, staring through the water as we lived with no care for time. That lake seemed to hold all possible dreams. I'd like to thank him for everything we shared.

Thanks to another old friend, Simon. Each spring he would arrive out of nowhere when we were kids, always the first to jump out of his family's van onto our driveway. He's still like a younger brother — maybe the closest thing to a Mosquito Brother.

Thanks to Craig, a great friend and one of the funniest people in a canoe. To friends in school years or after, especially Eric, Don, Blake, Aran, Joe, Chris, Doug, Peter, Katie, Angus, Marcia, Antony and Darren. Thanks to Linda, Lora, Bob, Michiko, Dan, Sun-Mi, Naomi, Wade and Professor Fudge. Thank you to Ellen Levine and Meredith Miller.

✳

In grateful and loving memory — George Grant, Minnie Kauffmann, Bronwen Wallace, Antonio Alvarado, and my cousin Eggily.

G.O.

MOSQUITO QUIZ

Test your mosquito knowledge with this True or False quiz. For the answers, and to find out more fascinating facts about mosquitoes, go to groundwoodbooks.com/mosquitoes.

True or False?

1. A mosquito can detect human breath in total darkness from a distance of more than 100 feet.
2. Mosquitoes are one of the slowest flying insects in the world.
3. The word *mosquito* comes from the Icelandic language.
4. The official noun for a group of mosquitoes is *horde*.
5. A flying mosquito beats its wings up to 600 times per second.
6. Mosquitoes live on all seven of the world's continents.
7. A single raindrop can weigh fifty times more than a mosquito.
8. Both male and female mosquitoes bite.
9. During World War II, a new species of mosquito evolved in the London underground subway system.
10. Many scientists consider mosquitoes to be the most dangerous creatures on the planet.